Moving People, Moving Stuff

Ellen K. Mitten

Educational Media

rourkeeducationalmedia.com

www.rourkeeducationalmedia.com

PHOTO CREDITS: Cover: © Erick Nguyen; Title Page: © Eddy Lund; Page 3: © Paul Vasarhelyi; Page 4: © Sean Locke; Page 5: © Jay Lazarin; Page 6: © travellinglight; Page 7: © Pierre-Yves Babelon; Page 9: © nullplus; Page 10: © choicegraphx; Page 12: © Jason Lugo; Page 14: © Nancy Nehring; Page 16: © CREATISTA; Page 18: © carlosphotos; Page 19: © cosmonaut; Page 20: © jondpatton, bakalusha, luminis; Page 21: © jondpatton, PapaBear; Page 22: © otografiaBasica; Page 23: © TennesseePhotographer, sgtphoto, shansekala;

Edited by Meg Greve

Cover design by Tara Ramo
Interior design by Renee Brady

Library of Congress Cataloging-in-Publication Data

Mitten, Ellen K.
 Moving People, Moving Stuff / Ellen K. Mitten
   p. cm. -- (Little World Social Studies)
 Includes bibliographical references and index.
 ISBN 978-1-61741-792-4 (hard cover) (alk. paper)
 ISBN 978-1-61741-994-2 (soft cover)
 Library of Congress Control Number: 2011924837

Also Available as:

Rourke Educational Media
Printed in the United States of America,
North Mankato, Minnesota

rourkeeducationalmedia.com
customerservice@rourkeeducationalmedia.com
PO Box 643328 Vero Beach, Florida 32964

People use **transportation** to move from one place to another.

To get to school or work, most people have to travel. People travel in cars and on buses.

People also travel on **trains** and on **subways**.

Airplanes move people quickly between cities and countries.

People also use airplanes to move **goods**, called cargo.

Companies use transportation to move goods from one place to another place.

Trucks and **ships** move tons of goods over many miles of roads and water.

Tractor-trailer trucks carry tons of goods over the roads from one city to the next.

Some large ships carry goods across the oceans. Others carry goods on inland waterways.

Railroads haul goods, or cargo, using the least amount of energy. Trains cause less pollution than trucks.

Computers connect all these different transportation systems to keep people and goods moving.

Which form of transportation do you like best?

airplane

truck

ship

train

bus

Picture Glossary

 **airplanes** (AIR-planes): Machines with wings and engines that fly through the air.

 **goods** (gudz): Things that are sold, or things that someone owns, as in leather goods or household goods.

 **ships** (ships): Large boats that can travel across deep water.

subways (SUHB-ways): Electric trains or a system of trains that run underground in a city.

trains (tranes): Strings of railroad cars powered by steam, diesel fuel, or electricity.

transportation (transs-pur-TAY-shuhn): A means or system for moving people and freight from one place to another.

Index

Websites

www.travel.howstuffworks.com

www.americanhistory.si.edu/onthemove

www.unionpacific.com

About the Author

Ellen K. Mitten has been teaching four and five year-olds since 1995. She and her family love reading all sorts of books!

Meet The Author!
www.meetREMauthors.com